Rusty and Friends

Marianne Parry

Matador
9 Priory Business Park,
Wistow Road, Kibworth Beauchamp,
Leicestershire. LE8 0RX
Tel: (+44) 116 279 2299
Fax: (+44) 116 279 2277
Email: books@troubador.co.uk
Web: www.troubador.co.uk/matador

ISBN 978-1784620-363

British Library Cataloguing in Publication Data.
A catalogue record for this book is available from the British Library.

Cover illustration by Dave Hill
www.davehillsart.co.uk

Typeset in Century Gothic by Troubador Publishing Ltd, Leicester, UK
Printed and bound by CPI Group (UK) Ltd, Croydon, CR0 4YY

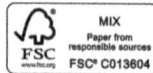

Matador is an imprint of Troubador Publishing Ltd

For Anne

One

Rusty's Dad

Sitting beside his mother on the back seat of the old bus, Rusty pressed his freckled nose flat against the coolness of the window, and felt the familiar sense of relief sweep over him as the bus lumbered away from the grim prison walls. He put his hands over his ears to block out the whine and clang of the heavy gates, sounds which still echoed in his head. Although he had visited his father for well over a year now, he still hated those gates, not only because they kept his father away from him, but also because whenever he and his mother walked past them, they made them seem so very small and helpless.

Rusty watched the fumes bellowing out over the busy traffic-laden roads of town on Saturday. He was thirsty. Rusty was never able to eat or drink before visiting Dad, and even though the Visitors' Room had been painted a bright blue to make it as welcoming as possible, Rusty's throat always tightened up and his mouth became dry. Somehow he made himself chat to Dad, and he hoped his parents did not notice that after all these months, visiting still made him nervous.

1

Right now he would have liked to ask Mum for another sweet, but he knew that it was very important that he should always appear patient. It was because his dad could never wait long enough for what he wanted that he was in prison now.

Rusty's dad was a thief. To Rusty, he was a kind, happy-go-lucky father, who often fetched him from school, and took him fishing, or to a football match on Saturdays. At least, that was the sort of father he had been. Even Rusty's friends had always followed his dad around, almost as if he were their father, too.

To Rusty's mum, her husband was also kind and loving. It was just that for some reason he could never stay in a job for long, so that they were always short of money. This was quite a worry to Rusty's mum, because she knew that whenever her husband wanted something for himself or her and Rusty, he would go out and steal it. Now he was in prison again, for the second time since Rusty was born, nine years ago.

She stole a sideways glance at her son, knowing instinctively that he wanted to moisten his mouth with a sweet, and why he had not asked for one. Silently, because the bus was hot and stuffy, she handed him a small bag of boiled sweets, and received by return a rewarding smile.

Rusty sucked a sweet slowly, thinking back to the long sleepless nights he had had when he had first learnt Dad was going to jail. His dreams had become nightmares in which his father was forever being chased down dark lanes by burly policemen, so that he would wake up hot and feverish and confused. It was after one of these nightmares that Mum had come into his bedroom and tried to help him see his dad as he really was.

"Rusty," she had asked quietly, "would you say that Dad has been a good father to you?"

"Yes, of course." Rusty had wiped away a hot tear with the back of his tightly clenched hand, but his mother's voice was so calm that he was already beginning to feel less tense. His mother sat on the end of the bed.

"And now, I expect you're feeling bitterly disappointed in him?" She paused. "Perhaps you're even wishing he wasn't your father. Perhaps," she went on, as he made no answer, "perhaps you would rather have Willie's or Sylvester's?"

There was silence, but despite the forlorn mist of Rusty's thoughts an unbidden giggle almost burst through at the image of Sylvester's dad, with his gleaming brown face and soft West Indian drawl, being taken for the father of a red-headed, freckle-spotted urchin like himself. His mother's voice, gentle though it still was, cut anxiously across his thoughts.

"Rusty? I'm waiting for an answer."

Rusty swallowed hard, but all he could manage to say in reply was a whispered, "No."

"Well then," encouraged his mother, "why not lie still and think of the good times, the fishing and football, and when it's raining, helping with your train set?" Her voice faltered. She had forgotten that the train set had been one of the many games Dad had 'forgotten' to pay for. Nevertheless, she went on.

"It's hard to understand, I know. Your dad is the best father in the world but he is also a thief." Rusty's eyes had grown enormous and gleamed despite the gloom of the bedroom, whose only light was the triangle shed through the half-open door from the landing. "Yes, your dad is a thief. The only difference is that he chooses to be a good father, whereas he does not even want to be a thief." She had stood up then.

"Dad may never be able to change, son, but he will try, and as dads go, he makes a very special one, and don't you forget it."

The next moment she had gone and the room was plunged back into darkness. Somehow, though, the darkness had gone from inside Rusty and he had turned over and gone straight to sleep.

Now, looking back, he thought she had explained very well, for he had felt comforted. Mum was right. He must never forget what a great father he had, and at the same time, he had to understand that although Dad hated being a thief really, he didn't seem strong enough to stop stealing things. Although Rusty accepted that his dad might not be able to change, his mother had somehow managed to leave him with a great hope that one day all would be well.

"When I grow up," he thought, as the bus turned the corner quite near where they lived, "I shall earn enough to keep us all and perhaps Dad will work with me. We could run a garage or something." His daydreaming stopped abruptly as the shabby bus jerked to a stop too. Soon they were home.

Two

Escape

It usually took Rusty a few days to settle down after seeing his father. It was always upsetting having to say good-bye, knowing Dad would be locked away for the night, even though during the day he moved freely about the prison for longer than most of the inmates, because he was a trusty. But Willie and Sylvester had devised a great new game, and Rusty soon became engrossed in finding and tying together long pieces of string. They rummaged about in the den Dad had helped them build in the garden, and they soon had three very long, though haphazardly knotted, lengths of string of various thicknesses.

The three friends squatted in the den in happy anticipation until it began to grow dark. Then with a quick look first to see if the street were clear, they ambled innocently along it until they came to the three end houses. They were old and their front doors stood almost on top of the narrow pavement. They were ideal for the boys' purpose. Gleefully, they crept up to the doors and surreptitiously tied a length of string to each of the three brass knockers, high and polished proud, above the three heads – one red, one black and tightly curled, and the third a nondescript brown.

Grinning widely, they scampered across the road and jumped the low concealing wall. Then at Willie's given signal they each pulled hard again and again at the strings, until the street came alive with the hollow rapping of brass against brass, followed almost immediately by the opening of doors, and the raising of voices in loud and indignant anger.

Rusty and his pals giggled helplessly until, hearing searching footsteps pounding their way, they scuttled around the corner and down an alley, already determined to repeat the game elsewhere!

If Rusty giggled more than the others, it was because he was still a little tense from his Saturday visit, but he was a resilient lad and after a few days he would return to his usual cheeky and mischievous self.

It was Tuesday before Rusty began to feel really relaxed. Unfortunately it was Tuesday when they heard the bad news. Two policemen, one a sergeant, came to the house just as Rusty was getting ready for school.

"I'm really sorry, Mrs. Evans," said the Sergeant in his booming voice, "but I'm afraid your husband has escaped with three others." As Mum and Rusty were trying to accept this news, he added, "And I have to tell you that a warder was badly hurt. It happened in the early hours of this morning. You will understand that we'll have to search the house, just in case?" His words trailed off in sympathy as he saw Mrs. Evans' face whiten, but she nodded quickly and then went into the kitchen to make them some tea, just as if they were ordinary visitors, not men who had come to turn her house upside down.

The policemen were quick and thorough in their search, even climbing up into the loft, and when they had finished they were kind both to Rusty and his mother. Rusty could tell that they respected her for her dignity. She was a gentle woman who never swore or used rough language, so that even the toughest kind of man was apt to speak politely to her. The Sergeant was the same one who had come to arrest Dad, and he remembered Rusty's name. Seeing the bewildered, hurt look in the boy's eyes, the Sergeant chatted to him in a deliberately casual way, trying to make it appear as though his dad escaping from prison was not such a tremendous happening.

But to Rusty, it was a disaster. He heard the man's great voice but he could not take in what was being said at all. His heart thumped away inside his wiry body, together with a sudden fierce anger directed against his father.

"Dad has let us down. Dad has let us down." The words went round and round inside his brain until his head began to spin, and the Sergeant caught him just in time as he slumped to the floor.

When Rusty recovered he was tucked up in bed, his mother anxiously bending over him. Immediately he felt ashamed. It was *he* who had let his mother down. He struggled to get up, but one of the policemen had stayed behind, and now he pushed the boy gently back against the pillows.

"You stay there for a while, lad," he said firmly. "The Sergeant will ring up your headmaster and tell him you may be in later and explain the delay."

Rusty glanced at his mother and she gave him a reassuring nod.

7

"Rusty, I'm sure your father went unwillingly," she said. "The men with him are violent types. Your father wouldn't be friends with them. We must trust him." Then she led the policeman out of the room and in a moment Rusty heard the front door close and footsteps going down the garden path.

He closed his eyes. Despite what his mother had said, he still felt that his father had betrayed him. Now the taunting would begin all over again in school.

"Thief, thief, stop him! Thief, thief, stop him!" Even his pals, Willie and Sylvester, had joined in some of the chants.

"Trod on a nail? Well, go to jail!" No, he couldn't face all that again.

Later he went downstairs and told his mother how he felt. Mum did not try to persuade him to go to school. She thought he needed a day at home to get over the shock, and she knew the headmaster would understand, for he had squashed the playground taunts when Rusty's father had gone to prison, and still smoothed the way whenever the occasional outbreak of teasing occurred. Besides, she too felt drained. Neither of them had the energy to clear the table and the dishes stayed there until dinner-time. Then at last Rusty's mum began to feel better. She went through the house, tidying up where the men had been, although they had tried not to make too much mess.

Rusty went out into the garden and sat down in his den. It was really an old shed, made of odd pieces of wood so roughly put together that it had a ramshackle look.

Somehow the day dragged by and when ten o'clock

came and there was still no news of Dad or the other men, or even of how the warder was, Rusty and his mum both went quietly to bed. They were so worn out, she with worry and concern and Rusty with his anger and hurt, that they fell asleep quickly.

Three

The Message

It was perhaps two o'clock in the morning when Rusty was awakened by a creaking noise. He dragged himself out of bed, his eyes still heavy with sleep, and peered down into the garden. The creaking sounded just like the door of his den being opened, but surely Dad would not have risked coming home now? Rusty stayed there for a long time, but he could see nothing and heard nothing more. Eventually, weariness came over him again and he stumbled back into bed.

The sun had been up for some time when he woke. He could hear his mother pottering downstairs. When he went down he wanted to ask her if there had been any news, but he was afraid of the answer, so he sat down and tried to eat his breakfast. To his surprise he found he was hungry and ate his cereal quickly.

When he had finished his mother spoke quietly to him.

"I think you should go into school today, and get it over with," she said gently, but quite firmly. Seeing his stricken face, she took him by the shoulders and looked straight into the hurt showing in his eyes. "Its just as bad for me," she said, and tried to laugh. "Just imagine what Mrs. Archer and Rosie Twithers will have to say when I walk into their shops! Come on, lad, there's only one way to face a storm and that's to walk right through it."

Rusty couldn't speak but he nodded his head. He knew that she was right, and if he didn't go today he would still be dreading going tomorrow. But he didn't feel very brave or tough. What if he cried, actually cried? What if he cried in front of Willie or Sylvester? But he put on his shoes and went off to school.

It was tough. Mr. Soames the headmaster and Mr. Roberts the class teacher had warned the boys off, he could tell, but the undercurrents were there – a snigger here, a back turned there. Surprisingly, though, his two pals seemed to be really behind him this time. Perhaps it was because they were older now. Sylvester fetched his dinner for him, and afterwards he and Willie played marbles in a corner of the yard. All the time, Sylvester kept his back firmly against the others, his black face set into an 'I mean business' look, whilst Willie, too, scowled at anyone who dared to pass.

By the afternoon Rusty was beginning to relax and on the way home, he was able to talk about it properly. He told his friends all that he knew. He had almost forgotten about the creaking noises in the night, but Sylvester who always had a lively imagination, was most interested in this part of the story, his face lighting up into a smile of white sparkling teeth.

"Well, come on." he cried. "Let's go and investigate." To his amazement, Rusty found himself laughing as they sped along the pavements towards home. But they were not in such a rush by the time they actually stood in

11

the garden, despite it being daylight. The boys knew the prisoners were armed with a home made gun. Since none of them could back away without losing face, however, they moved forward together until they were right outside the den door.

They listened. Despite the barking of a stray dog nearby, and the hum of the traffic from the main road, all seemed quiet. Even so, somehow or other Sylvester and Willie had gingerly edged behind, so that it was Rusty himself who actually opened the door a few inches to peer inside.

The den was quite empty. He opened the door to let in the light and Willie bounded in and landed on a pile of old sacks. Now that it was safe, he could pretend to be tough.

"If they had been here, I would have smashed them with a karate chop," he boasted, demonstrating by making slicing movements with the side of his hand.

"Pork chops, more like," jeered Sylvester with a grin, and he picked up an empty tin of beer and threw it playfully across the den at his friend.

"Hey, what's that?" asked Rusty. He grabbed the tin and the boys stared. It was the sort of beer Rusty's dad liked to take with him when they went out for a day's fishing. Rusty knew it had not been there yesterday. He knew too that his dad must have left it to show he had been there. Was there a message? He was too excited to look.

Sylvester read his friend's thoughts. He took hold of the tin and shook it upside down. There was nothing inside.

"Where did you find it?" asked Willie. "Show us just where it was, Sylv."

Sylvester knelt down and searched the ground where the tin had lain. Rusty grabbed a torch from the old nail on the wall, and shone its beam down on to the earthen floor.

"There's some writing in the earth," squealed Sylvester, his voice rising high into a squeak. "Look, it says –" He paused, because he couldn't read what it said. Willie couldn't either.

"In – er – im – er," he began, until he too dried up.

Rusty knelt down and looked at the word. His reading was not very quick but after a moment he had an inspired guess.

"It must be 'INNOCENT,'" he said, in his nervousness, forgetting to pretend that he had really spelled the word out for himself. There were two more words after that and between them they worked them out as, 'GOLDERS GREEN.'

"Innocent. Golders Green," they chanted together before dashing into the house to tell Rusty's mum. Later, when the Sergeant had come and gone again, Mum had good news too. The warder was getting better, and he had told how he had been attacked by three men and how Dad had tried to go to his rescue, but the men had made him go with them. They had dressed one of them in warder's clothes and he had driven out in the laundry van, as guard, whilst the others lay hidden amongst the clothes in the back.

Rusty felt deeply ashamed. He had doubted his father and he should have known better. His father was a thief, that was true, but he was not a cruel man and was never violent. His face crimsoned as he remembered how quickly he had turned against his dad, but his mother, as always, sensed what he was going through.

"It was quite natural for you to feel let down," she said. "After all, you haven't known Dad as long as I have. He would understand." Then she said no more, for although she was relieved that the police knew her husband had not willingly escaped, a new worry nagged at her. What if the three men hurt her husband? Where was he now?

Four

Back to Prison

Several miles away in Golders Green, the police were quietly watching a public house run by the brother of one of the escapees. The pub was in a busy part of the district and the Sergeant and his Superintendent had decided it would be best to wait until closing time, late at night, when all the public would be safely out of the way. For the time being, they were content to surround the building at a distance. Two men in plain clothes were up on the roofs of nearby buildings, a policewoman and one of the men were inside the public house pretending to be ordinary customers, and others, including the Sergeant, were hidden in vans and cars in the surrounding streets.

Sergeant Davies was not worried. He knew that each policeman had a radio and that they could all keep in touch and notify him of the slightest suspicious move. So they waited, as the noises from the pub grew noisier and loud voices, often raised in laughter or anger, floated across the car park outside.

Meanwhile, upstairs in the pub, three men nervously puffed away at cheap cigarettes. Away from them, sitting alone in a corner of the stuffy room, sat Rusty's dad. He was red-faced from the heat of the room and the lack of air, but they dared not open a window for fear of drawing attention to the room, which was really an old stock-room, empty except for odd boxes and one old table.

Rusty's dad closed his eyes. He was thinking of Rusty and wondering if he had found the message carved out in the earth in his den. He was worrying about his wife too, and every now and then he would worry about something else: the gun stuck inside the top of Ned Naylor's trousers. As he squatted there on the dusty floor, other worries came crowding into his head to join them. How was the warder? What if he died? What if the police thought he was in with the three men – a willing accomplice, in fact? What if –? What if –?

It was an hour later before his head began to clear slightly and he tried to think. As he had done many times before, he cursed himself for being a thief. He felt sick with shock and anxiety, not only about himself, but for his family. One thing he determined to do, and that was that if he got out of this escapade alive, he would make a greater effort than ever before to get a job and work for what he wanted.

His reverie was interrupted harshly then, as he heard Ned gasp as he peered behind the net curtains to look outside. It was nearly closing time and they would soon be on the move again. What had Ned seen?

The big burly man dropped the curtain and flattened himself against the wall.

"There's a cop out there," he snarled, his temper rising, and showing signs of quickly becoming out of control. "No uniform, but she's a cop alright. Arrested our Jessie a year or two ago. Know that blonde hair anywhere. Now what's she doing here, tell me that, will you?"

No one answered. The other two toughs just puffed harder at their cigarettes. Beneath their tattooed arms and hairy chests, they were just as frightened as Rusty's dad. How did they get involved in this, following Ned like a pair of silly sheep? Now, if they were lucky they would have to serve long jail sentences, and if they were unlucky – well, would they come out of this alive?

Ned's eyes were looking wild and strange. They were filled with a weird excitement, and Rusty's dad realised now that anything could happen where this man was concerned. He watched as Ned turned to the window and without warning broke the glass and began shouting out into the now empty darkness below. He was waving his gun around from left to right, ready to fire at the first moving shadow. Then he saw something, and he stopped jerking the gun. Instead a sly smile crossed his swarthy face, and he took careful aim.

Rusty's dad did not know what came over him, but he found himself hurling across the room in one great bound. He grabbed Ned's legs and brought him to the ground, just as the door splintered open and a huddle of policemen stood in the doorway.

"Well, hello there!" said the Sergeant with a deceivingly friendly smile flashed at the thugs near the door. "Time to go home, I think?" And his men led them away. Someone helped Rusty's dad up from the floor, where his tackle had left him winded and dazed.

"Come along, Mr. Evans. We won't be forgetting your

help in this matter. Your family would be proud of you."

Much later, in the very early hours of the morning, Rusty and his mother sat alone once again in their kitchen. Dirty stains still lay on Rusty's cheeks where the tears had rolled down his freckles. He had cried and laughed at the same time, but now he was worn out and too tired to go up the stairs to bed.

So he sat, resting his head on the table, and thinking of all he would have to tell Sylvester and Willie in the morning. But his last tired thoughts were of Dad. His dad was a thief. Perhaps he would always be a thief, but one thing was for certain. He knew his dad would really try not to be, for, all in all, he had not let them down this time. He had not let himself down either, and that, thought Rusty sleepily, was a beginning.

Five

Willie's Gran

Willie sat on the pavement kerb and scuffed his heels hard against its cold edge. His feet moved in a steady, unconscious rhythm and he was quite oblivious of the scratching marks on his shoes.

"Hey, Willie, them's your best shoes," said his friend Sylvester with concern. "Your mum won't be very pleased when she sees the polish scraped off the heels."

Willie glanced down at his shoes in dismay. Then he stood up and tried to appear unconcerned.

"I'll cover them with some black polish," he muttered nonchalantly, and then his face set into that far-away expression once more, and he was silent.

The two friends walked side by side along the pavement, kicking the odd stone lying in their path, but saying nothing. At last it was Sylvester who broke the silence.

"You been to visit your gran today?" he asked, knowing the answer already, but trying to break across his friend's reverie. "Bad place, was it?" he asked again.

Willie snapped out of his day-dreaming and gave his friend a strange look.

"It wasn't exactly a bad place," he sighed. "The rooms are quite bright and colourful. There are lots of armchairs and cushions and a huge television in the corner, but I don't know –" His voice tailed off. They turned the corner and dodged the traffic as they hurried across the busy road before he continued. "It's just that I don't think Gran is happy there, that's all!"

"Your mum told mine that the Home was lovely and your gran couldn't be happier," announced Sylvester in surprise.

"Oh yes, I know. All afternoon Mum kept telling Gran how lucky she was, the Matron being so kind and everything looking so clean, and Gran kept smiling and agreeing with her."

"Well then," drawled Sylvester in his soft Jamaican way, "what's there to bother about?"

"Well," answered Willie, his chin thrust out in his determination to make Sylvester understand. "Mum was chattering away, and Gran was nodding her head and smiling away as if she was the happiest old lady alive, when this trolley lady came in with the cups of tea and cakes. Smashing cakes they were!" he broke off, his face lighting up as he remembered the chocolate sponge Gran had shared with him.

"Go on," persisted Sylvester, impatient now to hear more. "Never mind the chocolate sponge."

"Sorry, Sylv. Where was I? Oh yes, well this lady wasn't unkind or anything like that. She was very pleasant really and she bustled over to us and handed Gran her cup of tea and cake. She smiled at Gran and said, 'How are you, dearie? Now, eat up and drink your tea while it's still hot!'"

"What's wrong with that?" asked Sylvester.

"Well, I happened to be watching Gran, hoping she would remember that chocolate cake's my favourite, see, and I saw her pull a face. I was puzzling it over in my mind, wondering what had upset Gran. Then it dawned on me."

"It's obvious!" Sylvester cut in quickly. "It wasn't so much being called 'dearie,' it was being treated as if she were a child." He thumped his hand down on his friend's shoulder in triumph, well pleased with his own insight.

"You've got it," agreed Willie, looking up at his friend admiringly. "It was just as if she said, 'Now be a good little girl and eat it all up.'"

They were almost at Rusty's house now. They clambered onto his back wall and Sylvester put two fingers in his mouth and let out a piercing whistle. Scarcely a minute later, the door opened and Rusty emerged, his freckled face still showing traces of the jam he had been eating.

"Race you to the den," he shouted across the garden to them, and the next instant, the three lads were stampeding over the lawn. They flung themselves against the den door almost instantaneously. Rusty lifted the catch and they were soon safely crouched inside on the old sacks which covered and softened the impact of the earthen floor.

"Willie's fed up!" announced Sylvester to Rusty. "He's been to see his gran at the Old Folks' Home today. He thinks she's putting a brave face on, but inside she's downright miserable."

Having explained Willie's long face in a nutshell,

Sylvester looked to Rusty for guidance. Rusty was prone to flashes of inspiration and the others invariably looked to him as their leader. He was possibly the most sensitive of the three and was all concern, as Willie described his visit over again.

"I don't know for certain why Gran pulled a face," declared Willie. "But," he added more firmly, "I am absolutely sure that she did."

"It must be awful," affirmed Rusty feelingly, "to see your own house pulled down and then have to go and live with a lot of people that you may not even like."

Willie's gran had lived in a house which stood right in the centre of plans drawn up for a new Town Library. It was three months since the bulldozers had smashed down her home and reduced it to a heap of dust and rubble.

Rusty went on speaking.

"Three months is time enough to settle in if she were going to. If she isn't happy now, she never will be."

Willie's face clouded and Sylvester's face copied the expression in sympathy.

"Poor old lady!" he cried mournfully.

Rusty was not one to sit and do nothing for long.

"Come on," he urged, "put on your thinking caps. We've got to rescue Gran from that place and that's what we're going to do."

Willie and Sylvester cheered up instantly. They both knew most of the thinking would come from Rusty, so they put their arms around their knees and looked at him expectantly. Rusty did not keep them waiting long.

"First we've got to call on your gran unexpectedly, just to make sure she really is miserable. Then this is what we'll have to do." He lowered his voice to a conspiratorial whisper. They were just ordinary lads again now, enjoying the air of secrecy and the promise of action.

By the time dusk had settled their plans were well made, and it was a much happier Willie who called a cheery, "Night, Sylv and thanks Rusty!" as they went their separate ways.

The following day was Sunday, so the boys were free to catch the bus over to Woolwich, where the Home stood in large and very pleasant grounds. The boys walked up the long curving drive, becoming more nervous and apprehensive with each step. Whispering plans in the cosiness of the den was rather different from putting them into action. However, since not one of them wanted to be the first to admit he was scared, they went on.

The front door was very wide and it stood open throughout most of the day. All the rooms were centrally heated and even with this main door open, the air was oppressive and stale inside.

Willie saw the lady who had been pushing the trolley, and just as she was about to ask them their business, she recognised him and smiled.

"You'll be wanting to see your grandmother," she said. "Did you forget something yesterday?"

Willie was grateful for the excuse.

"Yes, Mrs. I know it isn't proper visiting time, but I think I left my yo-yo in the big room."

"Oh, it will be alright for you to go in now," said the lady quite kindly. "But I'm afraid you won't be able to stay long, and your friends will have to wait outside."

This is just what the boys had planned to do anyway, so with a, "See you!" from Willie to the other two, the boys parted.

Willie walked on alone down a long corridor. Paintings on the walls were bright and small rooms he could see through open doorways on either side looked pleasant enough. Everywhere, though, there was a smell. Willie couldn't decide what it was. It seemed to be a mixture of food, cooking and medicine.

Since Gran was in good health and was one of the younger ones, Willie knew she would probably be in he lounge again. He strolled in and found her sitting near the door, in a quiet corner. A book lay unopened on her lap and she was listening to an old lady seated nearby.

Willie saw that the old lady was really very aged indeed. Her skin was lined deeply and her thin hair barely covered her head. He could see the pink scalp peeping through the thin silver strands. Involuntarily, he put up his hand to his own head as if to make sure is own hair was still thick and tufty.

Gran had her head tilted slightly towards the old lady, and neither was aware of Willie standing there. The lady was talking in a thin high voice and to Willie she seemed to be saying the same things over and over again. Gran sat listening patiently, nodding her head occasionally in agreement. Then Willie heard bustling footsteps behind him and he recognised the matron, mainly because her overall was a deeper blue than those of the rest of the staff.

She gave Willie a wide welcoming smile. Then she went over the talkative old lady and took her arm.

"Come on, Mrs. Splinters. Time for a nice little walk

round the garden. Mrs. Jones doesn't want to listen to your chatter now. She has a visitor."

Gran turned her head round quickly and her face lit up in delighted surprise. Still, she was courteous enough to wish Mrs. Splinters a patient goodbye, while the lady persisted in finishing her sentence before allowing herself to be led away.

"Whatever has brought you out here this morning?" asked Gran after she had hugged him. Willie tolerated the hug good-naturedly. Normally he resisted all attempts to be grabbed by affectionate aunties and the like, but he knew that in this case it would be very hurtful of him, so he suffered being almost suffocated by the lavender-scented woollen cardigan and grinned at her.

"Thought you looked fed up yesterday, Gran, so I brought Rusty and Sylvester along just to say hello. There they are, look!" He pointed to the two faces pressed against the window. The boys waved precariously. They were obviously balancing on one of the ledges outside, and Gran smiled as their heads kept popping up and disappearing again.

"Hello, Mrs. Jones!" they yelled in chorus, then "How are you?" Sylvester squashed his brown face against the glass, flattening his nose even further, and gave what he thought was an encouraging smile. The grimace made Gran smile even more, and when he suddenly disappeared with a yell, Willie was delighted to hear her chuckling softly.

"Why I haven't had a laugh since I don't know when," she sighed, then changed the subject quickly as she sensed Willie's unspoken concern.

25

"I must see about knitting the three of you a sweater each." she said briskly. "How would it be if I made them all the same with a sign on, you know, to show you are in the same gang?"

Willie thought that was a great idea. He forgot about the lavender-scented wool and hugged her.

"Terrific!" he cried enthusiastically. He was in such a hurry to tell the others that he almost left without saying good-bye. Then he remembered why he had come and fidgeted away for a few more polite minutes until he thought it would be alright to leave. Anyway, he knew Gran would understand.

Gran turned to wave to the boys, but they were no longer at the window. After Willie had gone she closed her eyes and tears rolled silently and slowly down her cheeks. Outside, three faces had now appeared at the window. They watched the tears roll down onto the collar of Gran's neat blouse, and they still watched as she shook herself and wiped her face dry with a firm resolute gesture. Then she got up and walked towards the dining room. It didn't matter. The boys had seen enough. Now they were totally convinced. Gran WAS unhappy, and they MUST get on with the plan.

Six

House Hunting

Not far from where the boys lived was a street of empty houses. They were due for demolition, but the bulldozers had ceased their noisy destruction quite suddenly. Rusty thought it was something to do with the Council having already spent as much money as they could spare on building projects especially with the government cutting back too.

The three lads sat on a wall opposite one end of the street and studied the houses carefully.

"There you are," said Rusty, "it's obvious that the builders aren't coming back. All their equipment has been cleared away. Well, which one do you fancy?"

"What if they do come back?" asked Willie doubtfully. He was beginning to have second thoughts.

The other two took no notice. It was just as if he had never spoken.

"I like the one in the middle, the one with the green door," observed Sylvester. He liked bright colours and this particular green was surprisingly vivid, considering the house had been empty for several months.

"Mmm," agreed Rusty, frowning thoughtfully. "It

would be a good safe place to be, better than on the end, anyway. What do you think, Willie?"

Since Willie had already voiced his opinion and had been duly ignored, he refrained from making a comment now. Rusty and Sylvester were unperturbed. They flung out their ideas one after the other, in expectant excitement.

"Mum says we can have our old armchair," offered Sylvester. "She thinks it's for the den, of course. I think she gets worried about me sitting on the earthen floor. She keeps saying I'll get rheumatism or something."

"What's rheumatism?" asked Rusty, puzzling over the word slowly.

"It's what old people usually suffer from, I think." said Sylvester. "Your joints ache and sometimes your legs or hands get very stiff."

"Oh," said Rusty. "Is that all? Now we have your armchair, and I can get that old rocking chair from the Scout's Jumble Sale. I asked Mr. Short if he would reserve it for me, because it was for a VERY GOOD cause, and he said I could have it for fifty pence."

Sylvester smiled as another idea came to him.

"Mum's just bought a new carpet for Josie's bedroom. I'll ask her for the old one. I'll tell her the den is crawling with beetles and things and we need something on the floor."

"Great," enthused Rusty, "and I can bring some cushions. We have too many in our house anyway." He paused and for a moment his face clouded over. "They weren't stolen," he assured them. "It's just that my mum likes to have a lot around, and she likes making them when Dad's away. She says sewing relaxes her."

At last Willie decided to join in. After all, it was his Gran, and their enthusiasm was catching.

"I'll bring some of Gran's own things. The ones she gave us because there was no more room for her own bits and pieces in the home. We've got them stacked away upstairs, all sorts of things – towels and tablecloths; knives, forks and spoons; tin openers; even a tea cosy or two." He brightened visibly. "Why yes, having her own treasures around her will be the greatest help of all."

All afternoon, they made their plans. They went inside the houses and decided finally on the house next door to the one with the green door. This was because the windows had been broken at the back, whilst in the house next door, they found odd pieces of carpeting still down, and fragments of curtaining hanging at the windows.

Rusty surveyed the scene with a sinking heart, but they could not back out now.

"I think we shall need at least two weeks to get this place cleaned up," he sighed. "I wish we could ask our mums to help."

Willie spun round quickly, his face puckered in concern.

"You mustn't say anything to your mums," he begged anxiously.

"Oh don't worry, Willie, we won't do anything so foolish. My mum would feel she had to tell your mum and then the game would be up and your gran would still be miserable in that home."

"Let's start tomorrow," suggested Sylvester, who was secretly appalled at the thought of all the work in front of them, now that he could see the mess and litter strewn all over the house.

"Good idea," agreed the others in unison.

"We'll meet here tomorrow," went on Rusty, "and the Operation Clean-up will begin in earnest." It was on this note of agreement that they finally parted.

Seven

Ready for Occupation

Monday came and the three friends spent most of it fidgeting impatiently at their school desks. The day seemed endless and Rusty, in particular, grew more and more restless as the day progressed. He was raring to go. All sorts of plans were racing around inside his head and he found it very difficult to concentrate. It was inevitable that his lack of industry should eventually come to the attention of his teacher. As a result, Rusty was asked to remain at his desk when the final afternoon bell rang, and finish the Free Writing exercise he had been struggling with since Break.

Outside in the yard, Willie and Sylvester were frustratedly skimming stones across the ground, until Sylvester spotted Mr. Burns the caretaker, and they sped away before he could detect them.

Rusty bumped into Mr. Burns a few minutes later, as he came dashing around the corner of one of the long narrow corridors. He saw at once that Mr. Burns was about to reprimand him. Mr. Burns' face was set into a grim frown, an expression that did not augur well for anyone who crossed him as Rusty well knew. But Rusty decided to get in first.

"Hello, Mr. Burns," he beamed, "I was just looking for you. I've got a problem and I'm sure you're the only one who can help me."

If Mr. Burns saw through the flattery he made no sign. His bony face relaxed into the grimace he thought was a smile.

"I can make the rustiest old boiler work, son, but I never was any good at sums and the like. You've come to the wrong man this time."

"Oh, it's not that sort of problem," answered Rusty, relieved to find Mr. Burns' good humour was restored. "It's just that we know someone who desperately needs some furniture and I thought of all those old desks and cupboards stored out in that shed in the yard. There wouldn't be anything there, would there?"

Mr. Burns looked down at Rusty's earnest face, the freckles standing out markedly against the white skin. He had a soft spot for the lad, remembering well how he had found him sobbing against the school wall just after his father had first been sent to prison. He had watched Rusty develop into a tough, likeable lad, who could now hold his own quite adequately against his tormentors.

"Well now, lad," he said kindly, "I'm afraid that furniture belongs to the City, not to me. However, my wife does have one or two small items she would be glad to get rid of, the odd stool, you know, and that sort of thing. Would they do?"

"Oh thanks, Mr. Burns, you're a real pal!" cried Rusty with enthusiasm, and with a cheery goodbye, he raced across the yard and into the street.

Willie and Sylvester were waiting for him on the corner.

"Trust you to get a detention tonight," said Willie indignantly.

"Couldn't help it," panted Rusty. "I just couldn't concentrate, but something good has come out of it after all," and he told them what had transpired between himself and Mr. Burns.

Willie was very pleased. They had a rocking chair, a carpet, a stool for Gran to put her feet up on, and some cushions to go behind her back. What else did old people need?

"Nights are drawing in now," observed Sylvester. "So we'd better get a move on." Then they sped across the road and went their separate ways.

Later that evening they were busy sweeping out the old house. Sylvester hated getting dirty and his idea of sweeping up was to brush the debris into a corner and leave it there.

"What's it matter?" he thought. "It won't be seen when the carpet is down."

Putting the carpet down was harder than they had imagined. Sylvester had borrowed his dad's barrow to get the carpet to the house. Despite being very old and slightly frayed here and there, it was very clean and Sylvester felt a pang of remorse, so that he eventually picked up a dustpan and disdainfully brushed up the piles of dirt he had left. That being done, the three of them carried the carpet in, puffing and heaving with its unexpected weight.

"Cor, I didn't think it would be this heavy!" gasped Willie. "I hope it's worth it," – and it was. Later, after much puffing and blowing and manoeuvring, the carpet was down. It was a quiet shade of blue, with small pink roses strewn across it. Willie gazed at it admiringly.

"Gran will just love that," he declared. "Thanks, Sylv, your mum's the best."

It was two days before all the pieces of furniture they had been promised found their way to the derelict house. Wisely, the boys had decided to furnish only one room. It looked quite presentable now and the boys stood back to admire their handiwork. They were grinning at each other in self-satisfaction when Willie suddenly shivered.

"Oh, oh!" he sighed, rolling his eyes in mock horror. "What about a fire? It's going to be very cold here in the winter. I'm cold now," he added unnecessarily, since he was banging his arms with his hands in an effort to keep warm.

Rusty was as optimistic as ever.

"Not to worry," he said. "We'll cadge one from somebody before Sunday."

Sunday was Operation Day. The boys had spent a long time puzzling how to get Gran out of the Home. Sylvester had suggested creeping in whilst Gran was asleep and painting red spots over her face.

"They won't keep her there if they think she's got smallpox or something," he insisted, but to his disgust, his idea was turned down emphatically. This time it was Willie who found the solution.

"I'll beg Mum to have Gran home for tea on Sunday," he said. "Then I'll ask Gran to come for a walk. After that it will be a piece of cake."

"There you go again," said Sylvester, who was unfamiliar with the expression. "Always thinking about cake, you are."

Willie ignored him.

"What do you think, Rusty?"

"It's a good idea, but how are you going to be sure your mum will say yes? Besides, perhaps you have to give the Home a month's notice!"

Willie shook his head convincingly.

"You two have been good as gold going to all this trouble for me and Gran," he said. "And now it's up to me to make sure our efforts haven't been in vain. Come on, let's go home. I'll get to work on Mum tomorrow. She'll be pleased, I'm sure. She said she'd have Gran home to tea when she had been given time to settle in."

So, full of excited anticipation, now that their plan was so near fruition, they went home.

Whilst they were eating their tea the next day, Willie's mum suggested to his dad that they should have Gran home for the day on Sunday, to give her a change.

"Good idea," answered Dad with an affirming nod. "I don't know why we haven't had her before. She's had plenty of time to settle into her Home by now."

Willie just smiled. He had been quietly working on his mum all day, dropping hints and bringing Gran's name casually into the conversation. All the same he was sure that his mum thought the outing was entirely her own idea. He could hardly wait for Sunday to come.

"Gran is going to knit me a sweater, and then she's going to knit two more for Rusty and Sylvester," he informed his parents, in between gobbling down his food. "We'll take her for a walk as a sort of thank you, show her our den, and we can all think of a good gang sign because she's going to knit one into the sweaters."

Willie's mum was pleased. His father was astonished

and glanced suspiciously across at his son. That Willie was fond of Gran he did not doubt but taking her for an afternoon stroll well that was stretching things. However, Willie gazed back at him innocently and then dashed off to meet the others in the den before he gave the game away.

Eight

Gran's Surprise

After what seemed a long drawn-out week, Sunday came. Sylvester and Rusty spent the morning over at the old house. Rusty had jubilantly commandeered a small electric fire from the school caretaker and the boys decided to put it on at once so the room was warm in time for Gran's arrival. There was just one problem. It did not work.

"What's the matter with it?" asked Sylvester in dismay. "Do you think the fuse has gone?"

"I don't know. Mr. Burns assured me that it was in good working order. He particularly stressed that he would never give away anything electrical that was faulty. He said that would be dangerous. It must have been–" His voice trailed off and a look of disappointment and understanding flashed across his face. He banged the palm of his hand against his forehead in self-disgust.

"Of course!" he exploded. "There's no electricity in the house now. It would all have been cut off ready for the bulldozing to begin. Are we stupid?"

"We sure are!" asserted Sylvester. "Now what do we do?"

For once Rusty could not come up with a ready answer. His inspiration had gone. Although they both wore anoraks, they were already feeling chilled. Whatever would it be like for an old lady?

"Well –" said Sylvester, answering himself, "We'll have to wrap her in lots of blankets for tonight, and tomorrow she'll think of something herself."

For the first time since they had first planned the venture, Rusty wondered how Gran would take to their idea. It hadn't really occurred to him that she might not approve. He was about to say so to Sylvester, but seeing his friend's thick lips pursed in dejection, he decided to postpone it. Nevertheless, as the morning progressed and they separated to go home for their dinners, Rusty began to feel more and more uneasy. By the time he and Sylvester had met up again at Willie's he was hot with nervous apprehension.

Willie's Gran smiled happily at the three friends. Although she would really like to have had a short sleep after her meal, she did not want to disappoint the boys. Instead she went out of her way to show them how much she appreciated their giving up an afternoon to an old lady. So she put on a warm coat and matching felt hat and stepped out with a determined stride.

"Hey, slow down, Willie's Gran!" panted Sylvester who was over full with steamed plum pudding. "I thought old ladies were supposed to walk slowly, with a stick or something," he added teasingly.

Willie's Gran gave him a playful tap with her handbag and showed no sign of slowing down. In an Old People's Home she might be for the rest of her days, but she wasn't having any of her old neighbours saying how fast she had gone downhill. She didn't slow down until they turned into the derelict street.

"This isn't the way to Rusty's house, our Willie," she said with surprise and a little dismay. Seeing all the empty houses only reminded her of her own cosy little house, long since reduced to a pile of rubble. Still, she had put on a brave face for the boys' sake, and she followed them without another word.

The boys could hardly contain their excitement now, and were half running and jumping off and onto kerbs as they neared the house. Then they were there. They stopped and faced Gran, their faces alive with mischief and anticipation. Even Rusty had forgotten his wariness for a moment.

"Surprise, surprise!" they shouted and before Gran knew what was happening she found herself crossing the threshold of No. 14, Winnowsty Street. She followed the boys along the narrow passage, hardly noticing the wallpaper peeling off and hanging down the walls, loosely swaying. She was completely bewildered and unprepared. Before she realised that the house had furniture inside it, and that some of it was hers, she found herself eagerly propelled into an old rickety rocking chair, a stool pushed under her feet and a cushion tucked carefully behind her back.

"Well, Gran, what do you think?" asked Willie proudly. When Gran opened her mouth but still did not speak, he hurriedly went on. "This is all yours, Gran. You need never go back to live in that Home again."

"That's for certain sure," interrupted Sylvester. "This is your new home now. Oh, it's all right," he added hastily, seeing an anxious comprehension beginning to dawn on Gran's face, "Nobody else wants it. It was going to be demolished, but Rusty says the Council have run out of money, and all the workmen have gone away."

"Of course," said Willie importantly, "We haven't finished getting it all ready yet. I mean, just for tonight you'll have to sleep in the rocking chair with lots of blankets around you, until we can get a fire for you."

All this time Rusty had said nothing. As he listened to his friends speaking, and looked from their faces to Willie's Gran's incredulous silence, he saw how naive they had been. For the first time he looked at the damp peeling walls and odd bits and pieces of furniture, and saw it as it really was. At last there was silence and the other two looked across at him for encouragement. Something in Rusty's face made them turn again to Gran. They waited for her to speak.

"Did we do wrong, Gran?" asked Willie at last. "We knew you weren't happy at the Home. We didn't have anywhere else to offer you," he finished lamely.

Gran looked from one to the other. She tried hard to speak but the words stuck in her throat and she found, instead, tears rolling down her softly lined cheeks. Although she was crying she seemed to be trying to laugh at the same time, and to the boys' puzzlement, at last she began to squeeze out thin chuckles and then sobs, so that they were completely in the dark as to how she felt.

It appeared to them a long time, standing there, that the old chair rocked its occupant gently backwards and forwards, the tears still running into the lace handkerchief she had retrieved from her handbag. The boys began to feel decidedly uncomfortable and disappointed too. At last the rocking and the tears stopped. Gran gave a big swallow, and managed to speak.

"I'm so sorry to laugh," she began.

"Whew, that's a relief!" gasped Sylvester. "I thought you were crying, myself."

Gran laughed again.

"I was crying, lad, crying and not crying if you know what I mean."

The boys nodded enthusiastically, Willie and Rusty beginning to understand, but Sylvester just nodding in happy ignorance.

"What you have done for me today, I shall always remember," Gran said, "but please, you mustn't be upset when I tell you I can't possibly live here. Oh, it isn't that you haven't made it very nice," she continued, seeing their faces drop. "I can see you've been to a great deal of trouble and have worked hard, but my home is at the Old Folk's Home now, and this house will be pulled down one day soon, when the Council have their next yearly quota of money to spend. If I stayed in this –" she paused and seemed about to choke again, "in this lovely home, I should only have to face the heartbreak of moving again." She looked from one to the other, holding herself in complete control now in her anxiety not to offend them. "You do see that, don't you?"

The three boys nodded their heads mutely.

"All that sweeping out for nothing," thought Sylvester. Then he spoke. "Well, what do we do now? You can't go back to that place."

"No indeed," agreed Willie, recovering a little from the blow to their plans. "We saw you crying. You can't go back there to have to listen to that old woman, with her squeaky voice, saying the same thing over and over again."

Gran stood up and put her hands firmly on her grandson's sturdy shoulders.

"Of course I must go back. That's where I want to be. I have plenty of company when I want it, my own room when I want to be alone, and no bills to worry about, no cleaning to do either. I assure you I'm quite happy there."

Then she explained to them that it was natural for her to cry when her family were leaving at visiting times. It was partly because of the pleasure of seeing them, a sort of happy sadness, not at being in the Home, but at seeing how her daughter had grown into a woman, and how big Willie had become, and how like her late husband he looked, and all sorts of looking backwards to the past.

Rusty understood at once.

"Old people like looking backwards," he said wisely. "They do make new memories, but really they seem to prefer their old ones."

Gran patted him on the head.

"Now will you take one sentimental old woman back to the comfort of her daughter's house? And remember today you have given me a very special memory to keep."

Her voice faltered and her lips began to quiver again.

"You're not going to cry every time you think of today, are you, Willie's Gran?" asked Sylvester anxiously.

"Oh I expect I shall cry a little," she said with a recovering smile. "In fact, I think I shall probably cry a great deal!"

Later that evening, after the boys had all had tea at Willie's mum's, Gran prepared to go back to the home.

"All those old bits and pieces of mine that you put in the house, are yours now," she said kindly. "I'm sure your den will be nice and cosy and next time I come here, I shall come over to see it, just as I thought I was going to be doing today."

Later, in Willie's dad's car, the three adults allowed themselves to release their pent-up feelings. Willie's dad had to stop the car and for a long time they sat there roaring with laughter, as they went over each little incident that Gran described. At last Willie's dad put the car into gear again and drove on.

"One good thing," said Gran, "It could have been much worse. They could have been trying to marry me off!" And with that they all burst out into happy laughter again.

"You are happy here, aren't you Gran?" Willie's mum asked hesitantly, as they prepared to say goodbye.

"Of course I am. Quite, quite happy. Oh there are one or two little irritations, but nothing of account." And with that they were all content.

Back at Willie's house, the boys were preparing to go their separate ways. They had stopped feeling foolish, and Gran's offer of her treasures had filled them with plans for the den. All in all, they were quite pleased with themselves. It had been quite a day.

Nine

Colour Trouble for Sylvester

Sylvester paced the quayside impatiently. The huge liner was already in dock and it seemed that an interminable length of time must pass before his grandparents would actually come down the swaying gang-plank. His Jamaican father, equally restless and impatient, had watched the manoeuvring of the great ship to the quay with only slight interest. He has witnessed it so many times before, and although he knew that endless formalities had to be observed before the passengers could disembark, he found the waiting period longer than ever before.

Sylvester pressed against him and for the umpteenth time asked his dad how long they had to wait.

"Won't be long now, son," murmured his father in his soft drawl. "Remember what I told you. Watch your manners and above all, show them that you are very interested in Jamaica, and in Kingston in particular."

Sylvester fell silent, brooding a little over his dad's reminder. He knew that his father awaited this reunion with fear as well as joy, and he knew also that it was because his dad had married a white woman. Sylvester thought now of his mum, fifteen years married and still considered an outsider by her husband's parents. And what about him and his brothers and sisters?

His reverie was rudely interrupted. He found himself pushed against the barrier by the surging crowd, which suddenly came as if from nowhere. Interspersed along the dockside, watching the unloading and loading of the cargo ships, the crowd had seemed small and thin, but now, as the gang-plank was lowered, they all converged on the ship, pressing forward eagerly as the first passengers began to alight.

"Pa, Pa!" Sylvester's dad was suddenly shouting now, and he waved his hands widely, high above his head. Sylvester, peering through the crowd of sailors waiting at the base of the gang-plank, saw an elderly couple whose faces he recognised from the photographs Dad kept at home. They too were waving and smiling broadly in the bright morning sunshine.

After that, everything was chaotic. Sylvester found himself being hugged and then being guided through the crowds until they were safely back in the car and on their way home.

Sylvester thought his grandparents seemed very friendly and affectionate towards him. They called him a fine boy, and wasn't he like Cousin Clive? He reflected that his father had been worrying unnecessarily. However, once they had arrived home, he was not so certain. As they entered the hallway, the grandparents greeted his mum coolly, with barely polite handshakes. There was no hug for her but the moment of awkwardness passed almost unnoticed as the younger children, soon overcoming a momentary shyness, swarmed around their visitors in happy excitement.

The next few days passed pleasantly enough. Sylvester's dad was able to take odd days off, and used them to take the family out both in the town and in the countryside, and even on one day-trip to the sea.

"What's wrong, Sylv?" asked his friends Rusty and Willie later in the week. They had just been talking about him when he arrived at the den in Rusty's garden, late and looking faintly dejected.

"I thought you'd be on top of the world having your grandparents come all the way from Jamaica," added Willie in a puzzled tone. "Don't you like them, after all?"

"I like them well enough, I suppose," said Sylvester without enthusiasm. He didn't offer any more, and all three friends sat in silence for a while. Sylvester tugged despondently at the loose, frayed ends of the old carpet covering the earthen floor, whilst Rusty and Willie squatted on large cushions. Their earlier enthusiasm for roughing it has long disappeared, and now the den was comfortably over furnished with odd pieces of furniture left over from their venture with Willie's gran.

It was Rusty who broke the silence. He had been thinking hard and with characteristic understanding, he had very nearly come to the cause of Sylvester's troubled face.

"Is it because your mum is white, Sylv?" he asked. "Don't they like you being paler to look at? Is that the trouble?"

Willie looked up in sudden enlightenment.

"Oh, I never thought of that!" he exclaimed. "Why, I think you're a very nice colour, sort of coffee. Nicer than being dark chocolate brown anyway –" He broke off in confusion as he remembered that that was precisely the colour of Sylvester's dad. Rusty stepped in quickly and covered up for him.

"They're bound to think it strange at first, Sylvester," he said encouragingly, using his friend's full name in his haste to help him forget Willie's error. "I mean, I expect they thought that your dad would never have to leave Jamaica. Perhaps they had their eye on a beautiful dancing girl in a grass skirt for him."

"They don't wear grass skirts in Jamaica, Rusty, you idiot," interrupted Willie, who had now fully recovered from his embarrassment.

"Well, you know what I mean," said Rusty defensively. "It couldn't be nice for them having to say good-bye to their son, and seeing him sail off to a strange land far away. My mum wouldn't like it, I can tell you."

"Oh, I know all that," answered Sylvester heavily, "but my mum's my mum and I don't like seeing her treated badly."

"Ooh, what do they do to her?" asked Willie, having a momentary vision of Sylvester's mum being whipped by a native stripped to the waist.

"They don't do anything," answered Sylvester, struggling to find an explanation. "That's just it! They talk to her only when they have to, you know, like saying thank you after a meal; and whenever Mum offers to take them shopping or somewhere, they smile politely but make an excuse. Last night was the last straw as far as I'm concerned."

"Why, what happened?" asked his friends in chorus.

"Grandad invited us all to go over to Jamaica for a holiday next year – just the children and me," he added in further detail, and pointedly not including himself as a child now that he was twelve, going on thirteen. "Our Cindy began to cry and said, 'couldn't Mummy come too?'" He paused. "Do you know how my grandma got out of that one? She told Cindy that she would look after her, and that Mummy was different from us, and she wouldn't be happy in such a hot country and that besides, she would have to stay behind to look after Dad. Do you know, I looked at our Mum and I could see she was almost in tears? Then Grandad went on and on about how beautiful it was in Jamaica, and how they would be able to play on the sands all day long, how blue the sky was, how beautiful the mountains, on and on and on and on. I just went out for a walk."

Rusty and Willie sat dumbly still, whilst all kinds of ideas whizzed round in their heads only to be discarded as of no help whatsoever.

"There must be something we can do," said Rusty at last. Then he whacked the side of his head with the palm of his hand in sudden inspiration.

"What if you were to pretend to run away, Sylv? Leave a note saying those kids from Blaney Crescent have been making fun of you because your grandparents are so dark?"

"What good would that do?" asked Willie in disgust.

"Well, if Sylv's grand-folks saw how prejudiced and nasty other people can be to Sylvester, they might see how unfair they are being to his mum," retorted Rusty, the freckles standing out on his face as he stared earnestly at the others.

"It might work," he added, as Sylvester stayed silent, weighing up the pros and cons. "You needn't really run away, of course. Why, you can sleep in the den here."

"That's the first place they would come looking for him," said Willie sensibly. "But we could take it in turns to smuggle him into our houses. That would be great fun. What do you say, Sylv?"

"What I say is Rusty's a genius – and you too, of course, Willie," he hastened to say, "and I know just what I'm going to write in my letter. Run into your house, Rust, and ask your Mum for some paper, will you, and a pen too?"

Rusty darted out of the shed, and was back almost before Sylvester had settled himself into the old, rocking chair with pen at the ready.

Sylvester's reading and writing had greatly improved over the years since Rusty's Dad was in prison but it was a good thing that Rusty had brought a whole writing pad, for the next hour was spent in vain attempts to say exactly what was needed, and screwed-up pieces of paper soon lay untidily at their feet.

"What if we get the Blaney Crescent boys into trouble?" asked Willie once.

"That doesn't matter," replied Rusty firmly. "They're always calling Sylvester 'Coffee Cup' or 'Chocolate Drop,' or saying silly things like, 'How's about you sparing us a banana? You's ain't forgotten how to swing in them thar trees, have you man?'" And he indignantly thrust another piece of paper in front of his friend and said, "Have another try."

A quarter of an hour later, Sylvester threw down the pen and held out the finished letter for Rusty to read. Rusty cleared his throat importantly and proceeded to read it aloud.

Dear Mum and Dad,

I am sorry if this causes you any worry, but I am leaving home. It's not just because of the Blaney Crescent kids always calling me names and the like, but it's because I don't like seeing Mum unhappy too. Something's wrong lately, and I have seen her crying when she thinks she is by herself. Well, Mum, I don't know what's the matter, but I'm going to get a job and earn lots of money to make you happy and smiling again.

Give my love to everyone, and tell Grandpa I'm real sorry not to be coming to Jamaica next year, but let's face it, it wouldn't be much fun without you and dad, would it?

Next time you see me, I will be a man, and very rich, and we won't have to worry what names people call us ever again.

Your loving son,
Sylvester

Willie was full of admiration.

"That's a really good touch about you being a man before they see you again. Makes it sound as if you are going to be gone for years and years."

Rusty too was pleased.

"That bit about your mum crying should do the trick too," he smiled, refraining from adding that the inspiration for that sentence had come from him. "Well, now we'd better decide when to send it."

"How much longer are your grandparents over here for?" asked Willie.

"Oh, they have another two months to go yet," replied Sylvester. "They've been saving up for years to have three months over here with our dad. Our dad's been sending them money, too."

"Well then, if you go missing this week, there'll be plenty of time for everything to turn out right before they return to Kingston," said Willie thoughtfully.

"Oh, let's do it right away!" enthused Rusty. "You know what it's like waiting for something to happen."

The other two nodded their heads in agreement, remembering the long, long week they had spent waiting to rescue Willie's gran from the Old People's Home.

"O.K." they agreed.

"We'll do it today. In fact, you needn't go back home now. You can sleep in my house tonight," added Rusty, "and Willie can have you tomorrow, because I can smuggle you in when Mum goes to visit her friend. And Willie can hide you in his bedroom when his folks go to visit his Gran tomorrow afternoon."

"What about my pyjamas and toothbrush?" protested Sylvester.

"You can borrow our pyjamas, and we can buy you a new toothbrush if we pool what pocket money we've got left."

And so everything was decided.

Ten

Missing!

Rusty and Willie waited until it was dark before posting the note through Sylvester's letter-box. Sylvester was already safely inside Rusty's bedroom, ready to dive under the bed at the first sign of Rusty's mum returning and coming upstairs.

The two conspirators had barely arrived back at their own homes before developments took place.

"Have you seen Sylvester today?" Sylvester's tearful mum asked Willie, having frantically knocked on his door.

"No," lied Willie, acting his part solemnly and rather well. "He didn't come to the den today. We thought he must be sick. He's been very down in the dumps lately. Rusty suggested he might be going down with chicken pox or something."

"Come in and have a hot cup of tea," invited Willie's mum kindly, seeing how distressed her friend looked.

"No, I must find him. Look, read this –" and she thrust the letter into her neighbour's hand.

"Wait a minute or two," she said briskly after reading it. "Our Bill will put on his jacket and go and look for him. He won't have gone far, not without this scallywag and

Rusty," she went on, at the same time throwing a suspicious glance in her son's direction. She called her husband, and a few minutes later, he had gone off with Sylvester's grandad in his car, whilst Sylvester's mum and dad went off towards Rusty's home. They were pinning their hopes on Rusty's den.

Willie was rather uneasy after seeing Sylvester's mum. She looked distraught with worry, but he kept reassuring himself that it was all in a good cause, and went back to watching the telly.

At Rusty's house the pantomime was repeated all over again, this time with Sylv's dad doing most of the talking, for his mum stayed in the car, numb with shock.

Rusty's mum offered to go with them, and soon the two boys were alone. Sylvester crept down the stairs and joined his pal for a feed in the kitchen.

"Your folks sure were upset," said Rusty in a concerned way. "Perhaps we'd better let them find you – after you've stayed with Willie, of course," he added, knowing how Willie was looking forward to having Sylvester smuggled into his home too.

"Hey, Rusty, what if they call in the police?" asked Sylvester, also having second thoughts.

"Oh, they're sure to do that, Sylv, that's obvious," said Rusty, "but they won't come looking for you here, will they? They'll be setting up road-blocks and things like that. They'll stop all the lorry drivers in case anyone has given you a lift. I expect they'll think you'll head for the Midlands."

Sylvester ate his cheese and tomato sandwich ravenously. In all the excitement he had had to miss his tea, and now he ate as much as he could as fast as he could, not knowing when Rusty's mum would reappear. He knew she would not leave Rusty alone in the evening for too long even though the friend she was visiting was sick.

In fact, it was almost two hours before Rusty's mum returned, by which time both boys were hungry all over again. Sylvester was unlucky! Supper consisted of beans on toast, and Rusty had no opportunity to smuggle any of it upstairs to his friend. The night passed uneventfully enough, Sylvester squashing himself into Rusty's bed as soon as Mrs. Evans had turned off her own bedroom light.

"Hope we wake up early enough in the morning," whispered Sylvester. "We don't want your mum to come in and find me."

"I've set the alarm clock for seven," Rusty whispered back. "Mum won't get up until quarter past, but we'll have to get you out before she comes up to make the bed."

For a while they whispered and giggled together, until weariness overcame them and they fell into a deep sleep.

In the bedroom next door, Rusty's mum heard the creaking springs and the odd stifled giggle, and gave a silent nod of satisfaction. She had been right. As soon as she had read Mrs. Grant's letter, she had recognised the paper Rusty had borrowed that day. She had returned silently to the house immediately afterwards, and a quick search of the rubbish bin soon showed Sylvester's dad the discarded earlier attempts Sylvester had made. Mrs. Evans had had great difficulty in preventing the Grants from rushing into her house there and then, but firmly she had pushed them into the den and spoken to them.

"Calm down, Eric," she had admonished. "You know and I know that rascals our children might be, but cruel they are not. There must be a good reason for this, or at least they must think they have one. I'll make sure that Sylvester is here, safe and sound, and then you can go home to bed. I'll keep my eye on the situation, have no fear. Stay here a minute."

With that, she had gone silently up the garden path to the house and stood outside the kitchen window. The curtains were tightly drawn against the dusk of the evening, but as she strained she could hear the unmistakably soft, thick tones of Sylvester's musical voice talking with her son. She returned to reassure his parents all was well.

Mrs. Grant was bewildered.

"What you say seems to make sense," she agreed, brightening visibly now that she knew Sylvester was safe, "but the rhyme or reason of it all escapes me completely."

"What's this about you crying?" asked Mrs. Evans tentatively, trying not to be too inquisitive, but anxious to help.

Mrs. Grant looked sideways at her husband, who still had a protective arm around her shoulders. He glanced at her, too, and nodded as if to say he understood. It was Sylvester's dad who finally answered.

"It's my folks," he said. "They are fine with the kids and with me, but as far as Jane is concerned, they just refuse to accept her. Oh, they aren't rude or aggressive or anything like that. They just make it plain that they will never accept a white woman as their daughter-in-law. Goodness!" he exploded, slapping his thigh in anger, "you would think they'd accept the situation after all these years!"

Mrs. Grant spoke up now, too.

"Even with the children, it shows. Cindy is their favourite, not because she's little and cute, but because she's so much darker than the others. But how and when Sylvester knew I had been crying I just don't know. I've been so careful. In fact, the whole visit has me so keyed up that unless I keep a tight control over myself, I could sit down and weep all day."

"We knew there were prejudices still," she went on, as the others remained silent, "but I thought that once they were over here and saw our nice home, and the children so well and happy, well – I guess I just assumed everything would be all right."

Rusty's mum took her friend by the shoulder, showing perhaps from whom Rusty had inherited his instinctive understanding.

"Then that's what it is all about," she said positively. "The boys have cooked this scheme up just to make your parents-in-law sit up and think a little more about their attitude towards you. I'm as sure as I can be that I'm right, though whether their action will bring results remains to be seen."

The Grants made as if to go towards the house to fetch their son, but Mrs. Evans wisely stopped them.

"Leave them be. Let's go along with them tonight and see what happens. I'll keep my eyes open and see that Sylvester doesn't stray too far. You two go to bed and if anything transpires, I'll find some way of letting you know."

So it was that now Mrs. Evans smiled to herself in the darkness. Tomorrow should prove to be quite a day.

Eleven

Never too Late to Start Loving

The following morning Sylvester and Rusty congratulated each other on the success of their plan so far. Rusty's mum had announced that she was going to the shops, which meant that she would be away for an hour, quite long enough for Sylvester to tuck into a large breakfast of cereal, toast and two enormous apples. Then they sidled off to the den.

"My mum never comes in here unless invited," said Rusty. "It's something we agreed upon when Dad first built it for me, and she has kept her word ever since."

Just then a piercing whistle announced the arrival of Willie. He banged the door firmly behind him and lowered his voice conspiratorially.

"Gosh, you should have seen all the fuss going on down your way, Sylv," he said. "Your folks aren't half in a state. I don't think your grandparents went to sleep all night. Mum said their light was still on at three this morning. Hey, you know, it's a funny thing, but I'm sure my mum thinks I know where you are. Your folks called again late last night and your mum seemed much calmer, and so did my mum too after they had gone. Do you suppose that means they've called in the police and think you'll be brought back very soon?"

"They were probably just too tired to worry anymore," said Rusty. "They must be numbed with the shock or something."

"All the same, we had better watch out for any cops," said Willie. "I still think this is the first place they'd look."

Rusty and Sylvester both agreed, but it was too early for Willie's parents to go to the Home, so they decided he would be better off staying where he was for the rest of the morning. As a precaution, though, they piled the furniture up into a corner of the small den, leaving a tunnel for Sylvester to crawl into should the need arise.

The morning was long and frustrating. The boys were keyed up for adventure. Instead they had to keep relatively still and quiet.

They heard Rusty's mum come back and eventually Rusty and Willie went home for their dinners, leaving Sylvester with a large bar of chocolate Willie had kindly brought him. He had also set out with a piece of cake, but had fallen to temptation on the way to the den, and had eaten every crumb of it himself! He eased his conscience, however, by promising himself that he would feed Sylvester up that night.

At last afternoon came. When it was all clear Sylvester and Rusty left the den, scrambled over the wall of the garden, and by the process of dodging in and out of doorways, and racing across the main road when it was clear, eventually arrived at Willie's. Sylvester now felt very unsettled. He and Willie only lived a few doors apart and he was too near home for comfort. He fancied he heard his brothers' voices as children scampered up the back lane behind the house, and for the first time, he worried about what would happen when he faced his parents again. Willie's parents seemed to be a long time at the Home, and when they returned, announced that after tea they would be going to sit with the Grants to see if there was any news. After they had gone, Rusty came back, tapping their secret signal on Willie's back window.

"You know, something's not quite right," he said. "I don't know what it is, but something's not quite right. For one thing, my mum seems to be remarkably lacking in curiosity. She didn't ask me where I was going as she always does if I'm out after tea. And she goes round looking – well, sort of pleased with herself."

"You don't think she suspects anything, do you?" asked Willie dramatically. "You don't think she's followed you?"

"No –" said Rusty doubtfully. The three boys dashed to the window and peeped out through the chink in the curtains.

"You keep back, Sylv," whispered Willie, so Sylvester obediently crawled away out of sight.

"There's no one out there," Willie said. "We're as safe as houses here. Come on, let's watch the telly!" And so they did.

Meanwhile, at No. 14, Sylvester's parents were closeted in the front room with Rusty's mum and Willie's parents. The younger children were in bed, and Sylvester's grandparents, unable to sit still in their anxiety, had gone for a long walk.

Their legs took them along the back streets of the

town, and then up on to higher ground. They climbed the hill without slowing down. It was as if they were both too preoccupied to feel their tired limbs. At last, their aching muscles sent persistent signals to their brains, and they sat thankfully on a seat to rest.

"You know, Marcia, this is our fault," said Grandad, as he looked down at the lights twinkling in the town. "We have made our son's wife unhappy, and now, because of us, Sylvester has run away." He shook his head sadly.

His wife hastened to comfort him.

"You read the letter, Reuben. You know what it said. Those boys have been taunting him about his colour. They are prejudiced about the likes of us."

Her husband interrupted her.

"Yes, just like we've been prejudiced against them." He sighed. "We – yes, you and I both – have set our hearts against our daughter-in-law. We have never forgiven her for marrying our son and we have never tried to love her. All this is our fault."

Sylvester's grandmother knew he was right. In fact, she had quickly become aware of what a good wife and mother her daughter-in-law had made. Deep down inside, she liked her and would have loved to have shown her affection. But respect for her husband had held her back. He had always been so strongly against the marriage, the mixing of blood, as he called it. Now she patted his gloved hand.

"Come on. It's not too late, and we aren't too old to change our thinking a little. We both know, I think, that our grandchildren have a good mother. We must use the rest of our holiday to show her that we think we have a good daughter too."

Walking back down the hill, their steps were lighter. If only Sylvester could be found safe and well, they would do the rest.

When Rusty's mum left Sylvester's house, they had agreed to go along with the boys' plan for one more night, but his mum had insisted that they tell the grandparents that he was safe, even without giving details. All agreed, for it seemed too cruel to let the old couple go on being anxious. Willie's parents suggested they should say that a message had been received informing them that he was coming home tomorrow, and with that decision agreed upon, the Joneses, too, went home.

Twelve

Success

When Rusty got up next morning his mother kept him busy with odd jobs, all of which he had indeed promised to help her with during these holidays. Inwardly fuming, he got through each job as quickly as he could, but somehow his mother always managed to find another task to keep him tied to the house. So it was afternoon before he could escape to Willie's house. There he found Willie equally frustrated.

"Sylvester's upstairs in the box-room. No one ever goes in there except at holidays and spring cleaning time," he added. "I haven't been able to take him up as much as a cup of milk. My mum's been under my feet all morning till you came. Now she says she's popping down to Sylvester's to see if there's any news, but she's coming straight back."

"I'll keep look-out while you take him something," offered Rusty. "I'll whistle the minute I see her."

Willie was half-way up the stairs when he heard Rusty whistling one of their school songs. He was back down again instantly.

"Is she coming already?" he asked in consternation.

Rusty's face reddened to match his hair.

"Oh, sorry, Willie. I was just absent-minded for a minute. Try again."

Giving his pal a withering glance, Willie ascended the stairs again and reappeared a minute later.

"Look up there," he said, pointing up the well of the staircase. Rusty looked up and spotted Sylvester's face grinning brownly at him through the cream bannister rails.

"Get back!" he called. "Here she comes!"

"How're Sylvester's folks this afternoon?" asked Willie, as soon as his mum joined them.

"Well, it's a funny thing," she replied, "but the old people have been a bit cool towards Sylvester's mum, you know, since they arrived over here from Kingston, but today they can't do enough for her. They're waiting on her hand and foot, and trying to cheer her up by telling her all about the holiday she'll be having when she takes the children to Jamaica next year." Tactfully, so that the boys would not notice the quiver at her mouth's edges, she hurried into the kitchen.

Rusty and Willie gave small triumphant whoops, but Mrs. Jones kept them on tenterhooks for another half hour before conveniently going into the garden to hang out her washing. The boys dashed up the stairs two at a time.

"Sylv, Sylv!" they yelled, "It worked! It really worked!" and they chased each other into Willie's bedroom and bounced up and down on the bed in their excitement. Sylvester's grin was ear-splitting. Then they remembered Mrs. Jones downstairs and reduced their voices to whispers again.

"The next thing is, how are we going to get you home?" said Rusty thoughtfully.

"Couldn't we say we'd been out scouring the streets for him and suddenly found him?" asked Willie. "Sitting unhappily behind a pile of dustbins," he went on imaginatively.

The others squashed him with two definite, "No's."

"Obviously, the best thing to do is for you to turn up and say you couldn't get a job," said Rusty sensibly; and in the end, that is precisely what Sylvester did.

After being half suffocated by his delighted brothers and sisters, patted on the back persistently by his father and grandfather, hugged and fed and questioned by his mother and grandmother, Sylvester thought it was time to find out if it had all been worthwhile.

Turning to his mother between mouthfuls of food, he asked, "Are you really coming to Jamaica with us next year?"

"Yes, she is. We couldn't think of her not coming," answered his grandmother for her, with a smile as broad as his own. "Say, how did you know about that?" she continued, but somehow she was interrupted by Sylvester's dad and the conversation turned to plans for what they would do and where they would go the next day.

Later in the week, when all the excitement had died down, Sylvester remembered his gran's question.

"That was a real sticky moment," he told Rusty and Willie in the privacy of the den. "It's funny, but no-one seemed to notice and I got away with not having to answer Gran at all."

"Mmm. Lucky that," agreed Willie.

"Lucky? I wonder," breathed Rusty. "Perhaps we weren't the only ones to have been clever."